W9-ASE-354

Let's Meet a Veterinarian

Gina Bellisario

illustrated by Cale Atkinson

M MILLBROOK PRESS · MINNEAPOLIS

For Sofia and Milla —G.B.

For my lovely lady, Jessika,
and my fish, Sashimi —C.A.

Millbrook Press
A division of Lerner Publishing Group, Inc.
241 First Avenue North
Minneapolis, MN 55401 U.S.A.

Website address: www.lernerbooks.com

Main body text set in Slappy Inline 18/28.
Typeface provided by T26.

Library of Congress Cataloging-in-Publication Data

Bellisario, Gina.
    Let's meet a veterinarian / by Gina Bellisario ; illustrated by
Cale Atkinson.
        pages   cm. — (Cloverleaf books. Community helpers)
    Includes index.
    ISBN 978-0-7613-9030-5 (lib. bdg. : alk. paper)
    1. Veterinary medicine—Juvenile literature.
    2. Veterinarians—Juvenile literature. I. Atkinson, Cale,
illustrator. II. Title.
    SF756.B45 2013
    636.089—dc23   2012022482

Manufactured in the United States of America
1 –BP – 12/31/12

TABLE OF CONTENTS

Chapter One

Even Tigers Say Ahhh!

Today our class is having a visitor. We want to know what a **veterinarian** does.

Veterinarians are people in the community. A community is a group of people who live in the same city, town, or neighborhood.

We invited Dr. Kate, the veterinarian. She helps us take care of Henry. Henry is our class guinea pig. He is also Dr. Kate's **patient.**

"I help keep **animals healthy**," says Dr. Kate. Dr. Kate gives Henry a checkup. She checks his eyes and ears. They look great!

"Can I be next?" asks Ethan.

Dr. Kate says veterinarians don't see human patients.

Veterinarians, also called vets, are doctors for animals. But their work can help people stay healthy too. Some animal illnesses can make people sick. Vets find cures for those illnesses. Then they share the cures with people doctors.

Dr. Kate is a **small animal vet.** She treats pets such as **dogs** and **rabbits.**

Small animal vets work in an office. Their patients visit them there. But vets for farm or zoo animals go to their patients. An elephant can't fit in a waiting room, after all!

There are also vets for **large** animals and **wild** animals. They help out at **farms** and **zoos.**

Even tigers say **ahhh!**

Vets go to a special school. They **study** how to **care for animals.** They learn about protecting them in zoos, on farms, and in your home.

Then they can help other animal helpers, like wildlife rescuers and pet owners.

Before people become veterinarians, they make a promise. They say the Veterinarian's Oath. Part of the oath is promising they'll be kind to animals. A kind doctor can be the best medicine!

Chapter Two

Hairy Henry

Yikes! What happened to Henry's fur?

He looks like Joy's fuzzy pencil.

Dr. Kate has just the thing for messy hair. **A brush!** She says it's one of the many tools vets use.

Phew! All better.

Some pets love getting messy. But knotty fur or muddy paws can make them sick. So vets groom their patients. *Groom* means "to clean." Vets trim beaks, wash hooves, and even brush teeth. Pet owners can learn how to groom their pets by watching a vet.

Sometimes an animal has problems with its **fur, scales, or feathers.**

A dog can get **bugs** that make its body **itchy**.

A lizard can get a **broken nail.**

Vets have **special tools** for solving these problems.

A vet's tools are made for animals. So they look different from the ones your doctor uses. Your doctor has a scale that's right for your size. But how does a vet weigh a mouse? A vet has a scale that's the perfect size!

Vets also use many of the same tools that people doctors use.

They use a **stethoscope** for listening to the heart.

They have an **X-ray** machine for seeing bones.

They also give **shots** that stop nasty germs.

Liam sure doesn't like shots. He bets most animals don't, either!

Chapter Three

Good Henry Helpers

No worries for Henry today. His checkup was easy. Dr. Kate says he's **healthy!**

"That means we're good Henry helpers," says Ella. Thanks to Dr. Kate, we learn how to take even better care of him.

Dr. Kate shows us the right foods for Henry. She talks about ways he can get exercise. But most important, she makes us promise to give him lots of love.

It feels great when your pet is healthy. But what if a pet gets sick? Good pet helpers call their pet's vet. Vets work hard at making their patients better. A healthy pet makes a vet feel great too.

It's a promise we *always* keep!
Dr. Kate lends a hand with Henry. So we give our animal helper a hand too!

Make a Dog Chewy

Pets need things like food, water, and exercise. These things help them stay healthy. They also need time for playing, especially dogs. Some small animal vets even keep dog toys in their office. Dogs really like chewy toys. Want to make a chewy for your dog? It's easy. Here's how:

What you need:
a fleece blanket or fleece scraps from a fabric store
scissors

1) Cut 3 strips from the fleece fabric. Each strip should be 24 inches (60 centimeters) long. The width of the strip depends on the dog's size. For a small dog, make the strips 3 inches (8 cm) wide. For a big dog, make the strips 5 inches (13 cm) wide.

2) Lay the strips flat. Place one on top of the other. Match the ends. Pick up one end and tie the strips together, making a knot. Pull the knot until it's tight.

3) Hold the knot between your knees. Braid the strips together. (Make the braid really tight. This stops the dog's teeth from pulling it apart. Then the toy will last longer.) Tie a knot at the end of the braid.

4) Give the dog chewy to a furry friend. Share a game of fetch or tug-of-war. Your dog will love playing with its new toy. And with you!

Don't have a dog? Bring the chewy to an animal shelter or a veterinarian office. Your gift will get lots of tails wagging. Wagging is a dog's way of saying thank you!

GLOSSARY

checkup: a doctor visit to check that a patient is healthy

community: a group of people who live in the same area

cures: medicines that help illnesses go away

exercise: an activity that a person or an animal does to stay healthy

groom: to clean an animal and keep it looking neat

guinea pig: a small, furry animal kept as a pet

patient: a person or an animal who is cared for by a doctor

scale: a tool used to weigh someone or something

veterinarian: a doctor trained to treat and care for animals

X-ray machine: a tool for taking pictures of bones and other parts inside of a body

BOOKS

Buckley, James. *A Day with a Zoo Veterinarian.* Mankato, MN: Child's World, 2009.
Read about the job of Dr. Karl Hill, a vet who helps animals at the Santa Barbara Zoo.

Salzmann, Mary Elizabeth. *Veterinarian's Tools.* Minneapolis: Abdo Publishing Company, 2011.
This book has photos of the tools that a vet uses. It also explains what the tools are used for.

Sweeney, Alyse. *Pets at the Vet.* New York: Children's Press, 2007.
Find out what a vet does during a checkup for a pet. You'll learn how it's a lot like a checkup at your doctor's office.

WEBSITES

American Animal Hospital Association
http://www.healthypet.com/
This website has pet care tips from veterinarians. It also has ideas for fun games that you and your pet can play together.

American Veterinary Medical Association
http://www.avma.org/careforanimals/kidscorner/default.asp
Visit this site to learn what pets need from their animal helpers.

Smithsonian National Zoological Park
http://nationalzoo.si.edu/Audiences/kids/
This website is from the National Zoo in Washington, D.C. It has real stories about how the zoo's veterinarians help a porcupine, a cheetah, and more!

LERNER 🖉 SOURCE™

Expand learning beyond the printed book. Download free, complementary educational resources for this book from our website, www.lerneresource.com.